D0475570

Where are my friends?

Edited by Kate Riggs
Published in 2016 by Creative Editions
P.O. Box 227, Mankato, MN 56002 USA
Creative Editions is an imprint of The Creative Company
www.thecreativecompany.us

Printed in China
Library of Congress Cataloging-in-Publication Data
Delessert, Etienne.
Fuzzy, Furry Hat / by Etienne Delessert.
Summary: A lonely bear who lives in a magical tree provides
shelter for countless animals in his fuzzy, furry hat as they all withstand
a deluge and become forever friends.
ISBN 978-1-56846-296-7
Animals—Fiction. / Friendship—Fiction. PZ7.D3832 Fu 2016 [E]—dc23 2015047476
First edition 9 8 7 6 5 4 3 2 1

Etienne Delessert

Designed by Rita Marshall

Creative Editions

A beech tree of a thousand years graced the garden.

Perched among the copper leaves was a lonely bear.

The bear sported a fuzzy, furry hat,

freckled with ribbons and bells.

Nice music ...

I like this fuzzy grass.

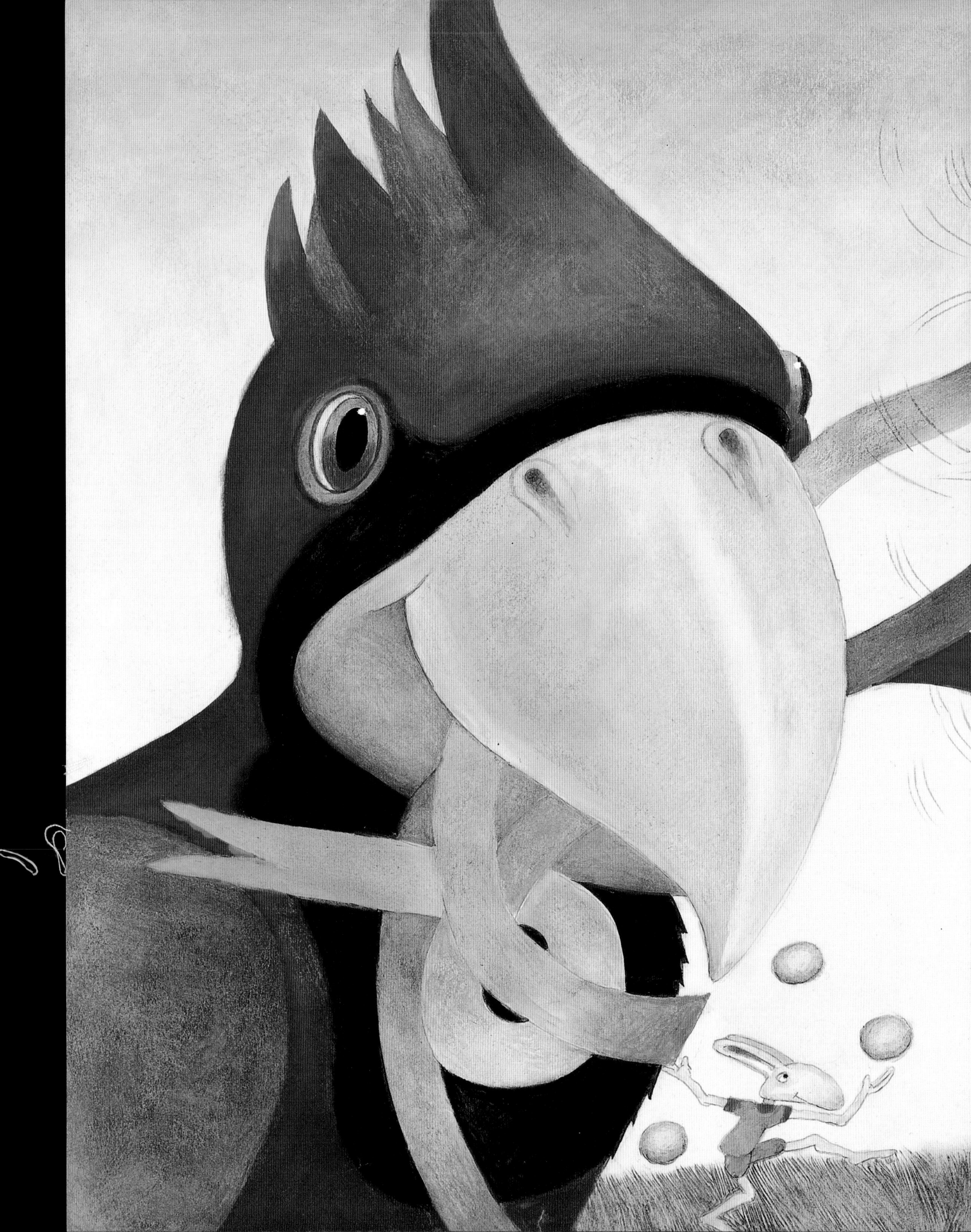

But is something moving?

This looks like a soft place to build a nest.

As the bells rang,
more animals followed.

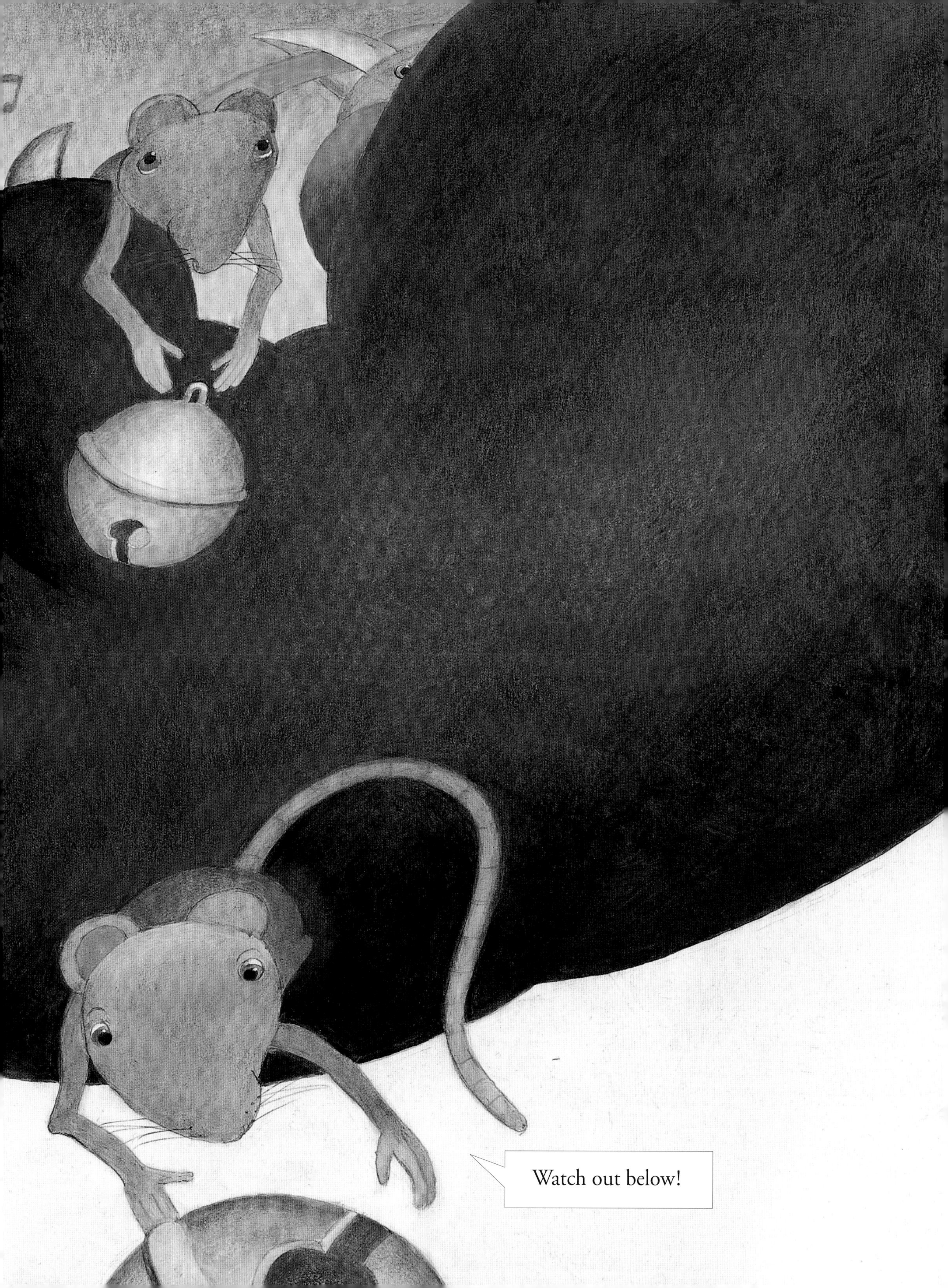
Watch out below!

And the music rang 'round the world

as the bear welcomed his new friends.

Oof, steep climb ...
It's crowded! Move over!

But slowly the sky grew dark.

Bear: Uh-oh, I felt a drop on my hat...

Duck: Who cares? Water slips off my feathers.

Frog: I needed a bath.

Snail: !

Pig: I love mud!

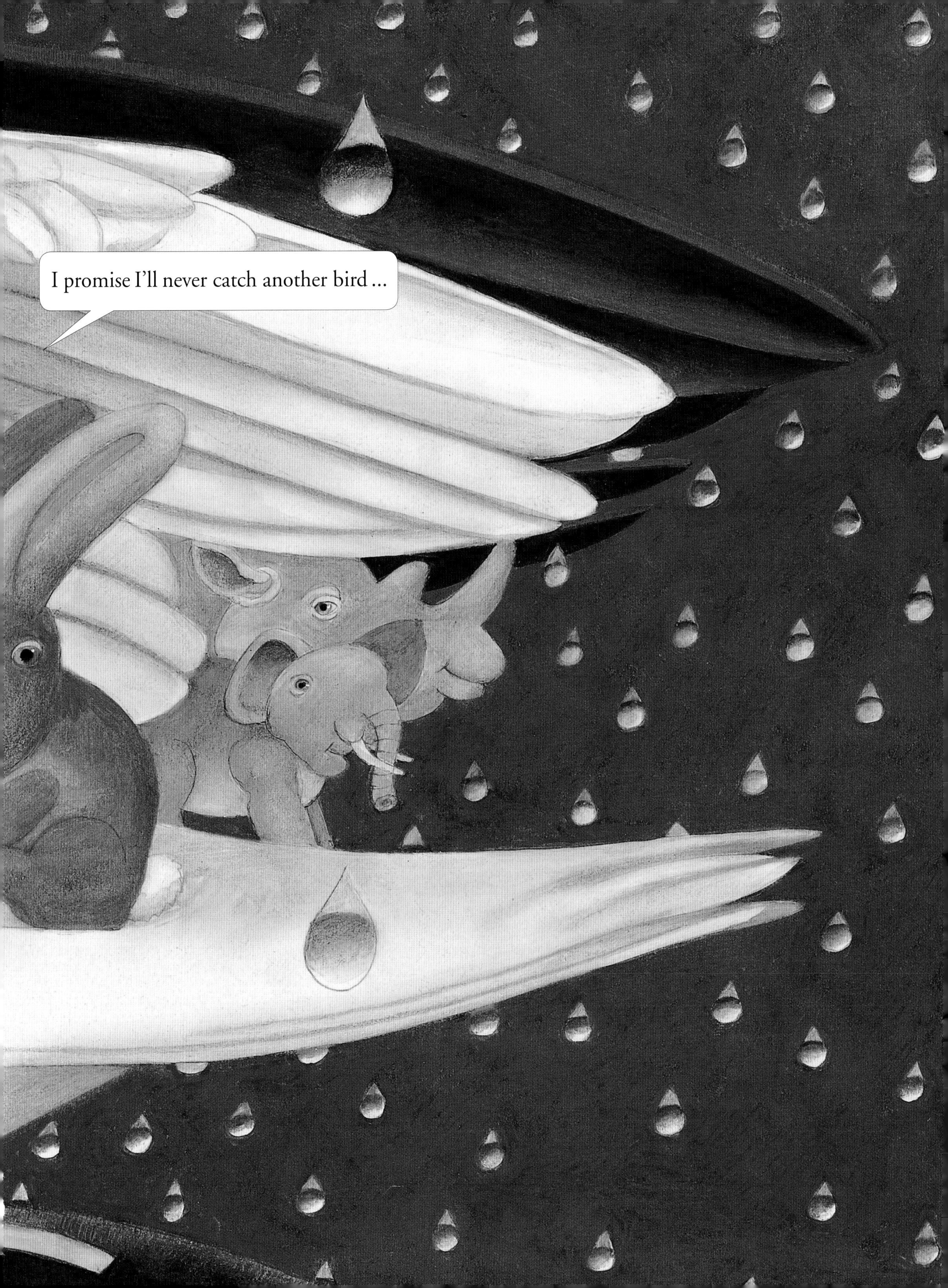
I promise I'll never catch another bird ...

The rain fell for months,
yet the copper beech stood a thousand miles tall.

Until one day, …

... music filled the skies once again.

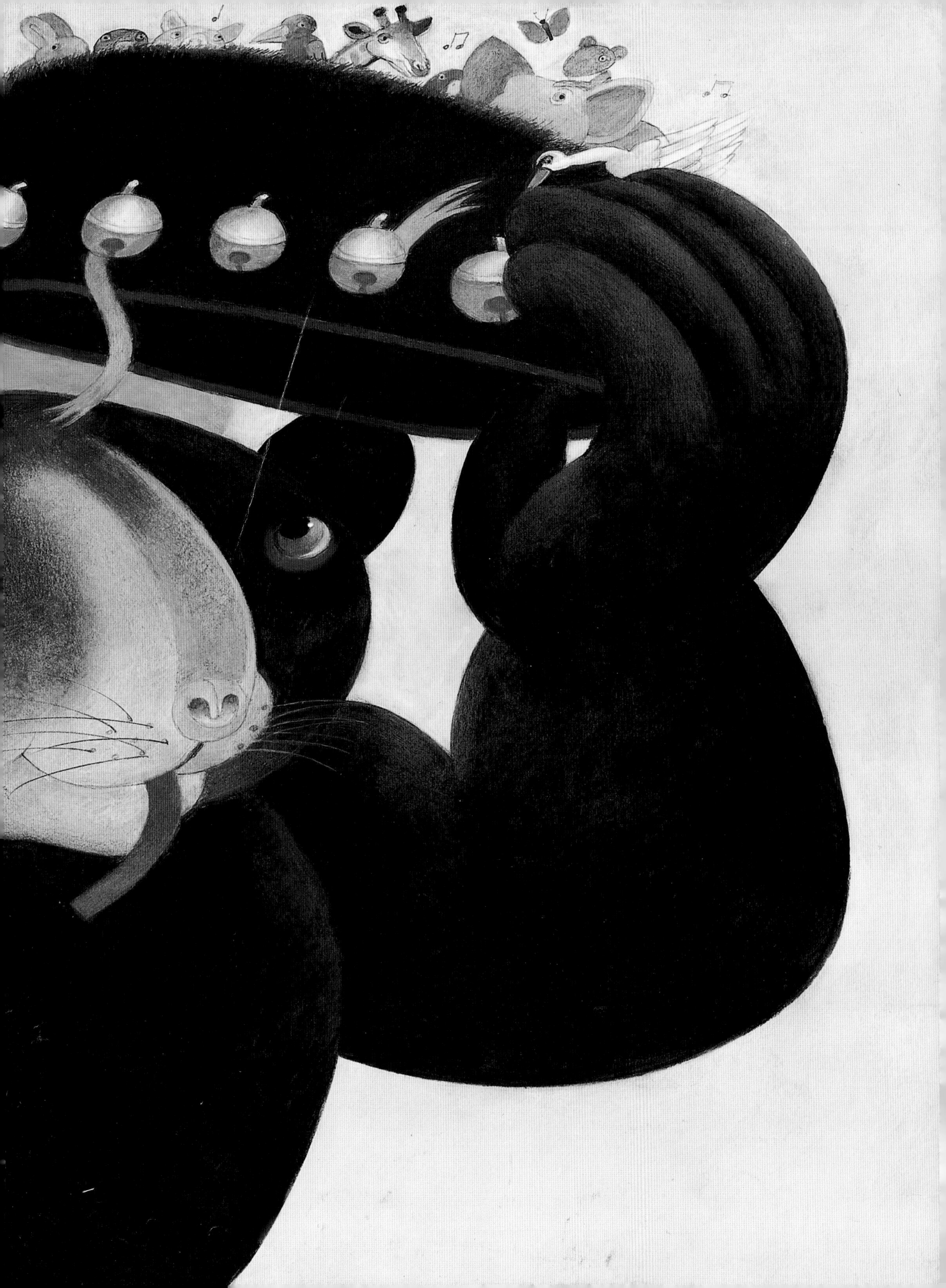